Revised Edition

Tom Brady

By Jeff Savage

AMAZING ATHLETES

Lerner Publications Company • Minneapolis

For Bailey Savage—as cool as Tom Brady

Lerner Publications Company
A division of Lerner Publishing Group, Inc.
241 First Avenue North
Minneapolis, Minnesota 55401 U.S.A.

Website address: www.lernerbooks.com

Library of Congress Cataloging-in-Publication Data

Savage, Jeff, 1961–
Tom Brady / by Jeff Savage. — Rev. ed.
    p.   cm. — (Amazing athletes)
Includes bibliographical references and index.
ISBN 978-0-7613-4215-1 (pbk. : alk. paper)
1. Brady, Tom, 1977– —Juvenile literature. 2. Football players—United States—Biography—Juvenile literature. I. Title.
GV939.B685S38 2009
796.332092—dc22   2008016096
[B]

Manufactured in the United States of America
1 2 3 4 5 6 – BP – 14 13 12 11 10 09

TABLE OF CONTENTS

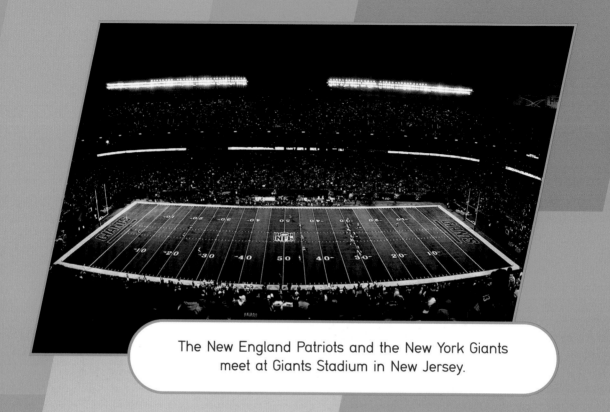

The New England Patriots and the New York Giants meet at Giants Stadium in New Jersey.

"TRUST IN TOM"

In December 2007, the Patriots and the Giants were starting the second half of an historic football game. If the Pats won, they'd be the first team to go 16-0 in the **regular season**. But the Patriots were losing 21–16. And the Giants were playing some of their best football yet. The announcers wondered what Bill Belichick, the Pats coach, said at **halftime**. Announcer Cris Collinsworth guessed Belichick had said "Trust in Tom." Tom meant Pats **quarterback** Tom Brady. His teammates knew he was calm in the huddle. If any quarterback could bring them a win from behind, it was Tom.

Tom runs onto the field to help bring his team a victory against the Giants.

But the team had to get to work. The Giants' defense was playing tough. And its offense was continuing to score. Early in the third quarter, the Giants notched another **touchdown**. The score was 28–16. Tom answered with a touchdown late in the quarter. The Pats were still down, 28–23.

In the fourth quarter, Tom threw a long bomb to **wide receiver** Randy Moss. Moss dropped the

The Giants' defense played well against the Patriots.

Randy Moss outruns the Giants' defense for a touchdown.

pass. But Tom went right back to the quick receiver on the next play. Tom's 65-yard pass sailed into Moss's hands. With this pass, Tom reached another important mark. He broke the league record for touchdown passes in a regular season. Moss's catch gave him the record for receiving touchdowns.

More important for the team, though, the pass resulted in a touchdown. A **two-point conversion** gave the Pats the lead, 31–28. On the next play, a Pats **interception** put the ball back in Tom's hands. He peppered the field with throws, until a running play gave the Pats another touchdown. The score was 38–28.

But the Giants came roaring back. They got another touchdown with about a minute left in the game. The score was 38–35. The Giants had to

The Miami Dolphins had won all of their regular season games in 1972. But the season was only 14 games long at that time. They also won all three of their **playoff** games, including the **Super Bowl**. The Dolphins became the only team to have a perfect regular and playoff season, going 17–0 in all.

kick the ball to the Patriots. The Giants' chose to make an **onside kick**. This type of kick is often low and short. The receiving team sometimes can't hold on to the ball. So the kicking team is able to scramble and get the ball back. This time, though, the Pats' Mike Vrabel held on tight. Tom and his team ran out the clock and entered the record books.

Fans of the Patriots were thrilled by the team's perfect regular season.

Tom grew up near San Francisco in the 1980s. At that time, San Francisco quarterback Joe Montana (*above*) was at the top of his game.

LEARNING TO COMPETE

Tom was born August 3, 1977. He was the fourth child of Tom Sr. and Galynn Brady. The Bradys lived in San Mateo, a city near San Francisco, California. Tom was the baby brother to three sisters—Maureen, Julie, and Nancy. The entire family was crazy about sports.

Tom's boyhood hero was Joe Montana. During the 1980s, Montana was the **Super Bowl**-winning quarterback of the San Francisco 49ers. Just like Montana, Tom was not especially big or fast. But he loved to play sports. By age six, Tom was challenging older boys to run races.

Tom hated to lose. And sometimes he was not a good sport about losing. He threw his video game controller at the TV. He smashed his tennis racket on the court. "It got to where nobody wanted to play with me," he said.

In 1991, when Tom was fourteen, he started going to Junipero Serra High School. By this time, he'd learned to control his emotions. Serra High was known for its sports programs. Tom played catcher on the school's baseball team. But football was Tom's favorite sport.

Tom *(left)* stretches to tag out a player during a baseball game at Serra High.

In addition to daily practice, Tom created a tough workout program to stay in shape. Tom threw for nearly 4,000 yards and 31 touchdowns during high school. His skills drew the attention of more than 75 colleges around the country.

Tom was also a talented baseball player. The Montreal Expos picked him in the 1995 baseball draft. But Tom chose to go to college and play football.

Waiting His Turn

In 1995, at age seventeen, Tom sorted through his **scholarship** offers. He chose the University of Michigan, whose team name is the Wolverines. He moved away from home and became Michigan's **third-string** quarterback. College was fun for Tom, but he didn't get to play his first two years. He grew frustrated.

"I turned into a whiner," Tom admitted. He told his coach, Lloyd Carr, that he wanted to transfer to the University of California. Coach Carr convinced Tom not to give up. "Just put everything else out of your mind and worry about making yourself better," he told his young player.

Tom did as his coach told him. In 1998, in his third year, he became the team's starting quarterback. Over the next two years, Tom guided the Wolverines to a record of 20 wins and 5 losses. Tom's final college pass was a game-winning touchdown. It earned the Wolverines a dramatic 35–34 win over the University of Alabama in the Orange Bowl.

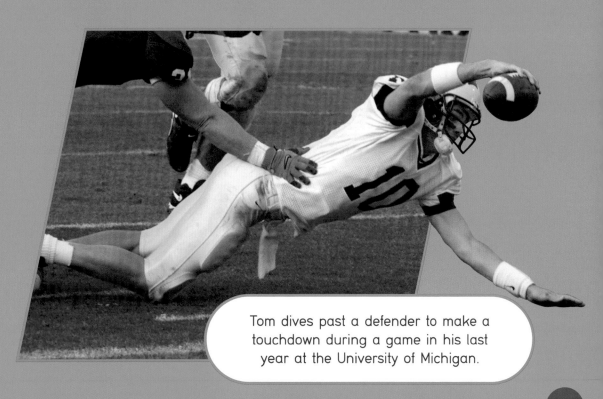

Tom dives past a defender to make a touchdown during a game in his last year at the University of Michigan.

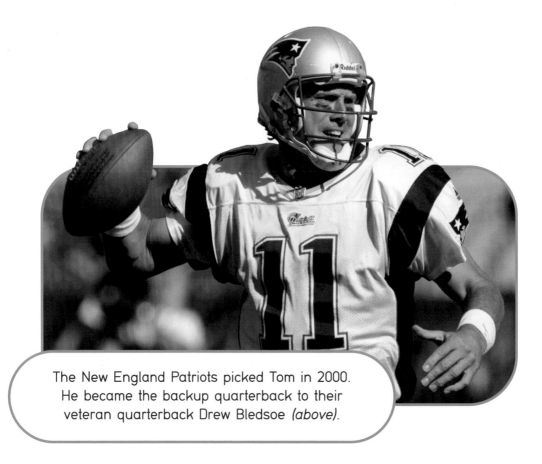

The New England Patriots picked Tom in 2000. He became the backup quarterback to their veteran quarterback Drew Bledsoe *(above)*.

But during the 2000 National Football League (NFL) **Draft**, coaches were not impressed. Tom wasn't drafted until the New England Patriots took him in the sixth round. He was very disappointed.

He joined the New England Patriots as a **rookie** quarterback. He would back up the team's **veteran** quarterback Drew Bledsoe.

In the 2000 season, Tom watched the Patriots finish last in their **division**. For the year, he completed just one pass for six yards. But Tom didn't pout. Instead, he worked harder. He practiced his footwork and memorized the team's **playbook**.

The 2001 season began badly. The Patriots lost their first two games. During the second loss, Bledsoe suffered a serious chest injury. He would be out for the season. Coach Belichick told Tom he was going to start the third game.

Patriots' head coach Bill Belichick noticed Tom squeezed the ball with a hard grip. This grip allowed him to throw a tight spiral. But this way of throwing also meant he didn't throw the ball very far. Tight spirals tend to be more on target. Tom liked being an accurate passer rather than a long passer.

Snow was a factor in one famous playoff game against the Oakland Raiders. Slipping and sliding, Tom narrowly escapes a bunch of defenders to get a touchdown.

SEIZING THE MOMENT

Tom seized the chance. He was careful and smart. In fact, he didn't throw an interception in his first 162 pass attempts. This was an NFL record. He led the Patriots to 11 wins in 14 games and into the **playoffs**.

In the first playoff game, New England played the Oakland Raiders at the Patriots' stadium in Foxboro, Massachusetts. It was January 2002, and snow blanketed the field. Playing was tough. At the end of the fourth quarter, the Patriots tied the game with a field goal. The game went into **overtime.** Tom marched his team close enough for the kicker to make another field goal and win the game.

Patriots' kicker Adam Vinatieri raises his fist in celebration. He'd just kicked a field goal to defeat the Raiders in the playoffs.

A week later, the Patriots upset the Pittsburgh Steelers to reach the Super Bowl. Everyone was asking, who is this kid Tom Brady?

The Patriots weren't favored to win the Super Bowl. They'd be playing the high-powered St. Louis Rams.

Before playing in the Super Bowl in 2002, some of Tom's teammates paced the locker room. Others studied the game plan. What was Tom doing? He was stretched out on the floor taking a nap!

One by one, the Rams' major players ran onto the field. The Patriots came out in one big group—as a team. This was the way they wanted to play.

Tom kept his cool in the game. The Patriots carried a 17–3 lead into the fourth quarter. But the Rams stormed back to tie the game.

Tom gets out of trouble during Super Bowl XXXVI against the St. Louis Rams.

The Patriots had no timeouts left. Only 1:21 was left on the clock. Tom dodged defenders and completed a pass. Then he completed another. Calmly, he hurried his team. With three more passes, he moved the Patriots to the Rams' 30-yard line.

With seven seconds left on the clock, Adam Vinatieri *(left)* came through with a 48-yard field goal. Tom was the youngest quarterback to win a Super Bowl. He was also the youngest MVP.

Seven seconds remained. Vinatieri lined up for a field goal. The ball sailed through the uprights for a stunning victory! Tom was named the game's most valuable player (MVP). "Incredible," said Tom. "That's why you keep working hard."

Tom's next stop after his win was a trip to Disney World in Florida!

CALIFORNIA COOL

Tom's life changed suddenly. As the game's MVP, he was flown to Disney World. He returned to Boston, Massachusetts, for the team's victory parade. Then he flew to Hawaii to play in the **Pro Bowl**.

He played golf with football great Dan Marino. He hung out with baseball stars Barry Bonds and Willie Mays. He got so many phone calls that he had to change his telephone number—three times. Tom admitted that all the attention was wearing him out.

At the same time, Bledsoe was traded. The Patriots had become Tom's team. He finished the

Tom *(left)* traded golf tips with former Miami Dolphins quarterback Dan Marino.

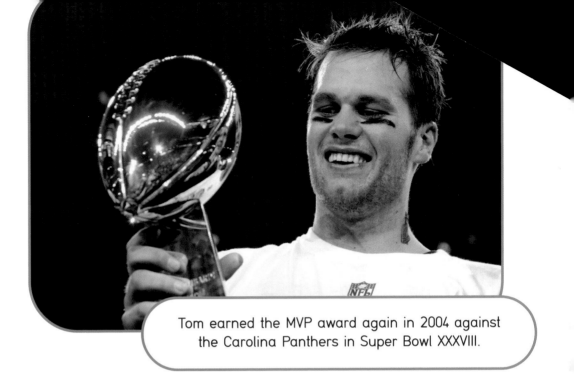

Tom earned the MVP award again in 2004 against the Carolina Panthers in Super Bowl XXXVIII.

2002 season with more touchdown passes than any other quarterback. But the Patriots finished with a 9–7 record and missed the playoffs. Tom was determined not to let that happen again.

New England opened the 2003 season with a 31–0 loss to the Buffalo Bills. Then the Patriots won 17 of their next 18 games. They ended their season with their second Super Bowl victory in three years. Tom was an easy choice for Super Bowl MVP again.

e Patriots kept up their winning pace in e 2004 season. They reached the playoffs by beating the Indianapolis Colts and the Pittsburgh Steelers. They capped the season by winning their third Super Bowl in four years. After the season, the Patriots gave Tom a new six-year contract worth $60 million.

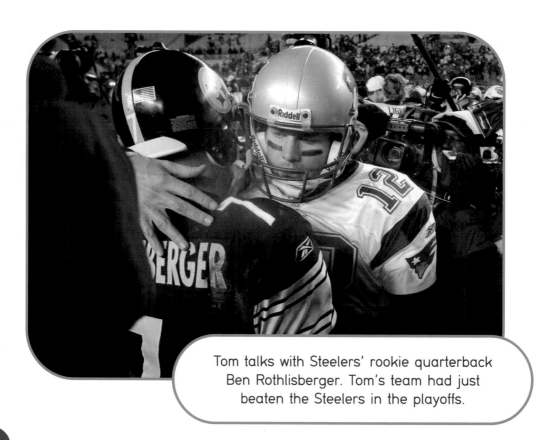

Tom talks with Steelers' rookie quarterback Ben Rothlisberger. Tom's team had just beaten the Steelers in the playoffs.

The team got bumped from the playoffs in 2005 and 2006. Tom was frustrated. The 2007 season brought in some new faces. One new Patriot was receiver Randy Moss. Another was Wes Welker. The team started the regular season with some blowout wins. Tom was hitting Moss and Welker with some amazing passes. By midseason, the team was 8–0. They struggled in some games in the second half of the season. But they still squeaked out wins. Their last regular season win over the Giants gave them

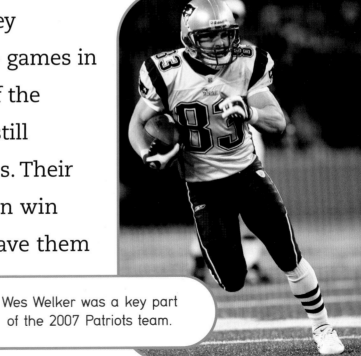

Wes Welker was a key part of the 2007 Patriots team.

a 16–0 season. Tom was the easy choice for league MVP.

As the Patriots headed into the playoffs, the buzz got louder. Would they go all the way to match the Dolphins' 1972 record? They won two playoff games to get to the Super Bowl. There they met the Giants, who'd played hard to reach the big game. And the Patriots knew the Giants didn't give up. The game was tight throughout. But in the end, the Giants pulled out the win, 17–14. Tom was gracious in defeat. But he's already looking toward the 2008 season.

Tom has been compared to Joe Montana, his boyhood idol. Montana's nickname was Joe Cool. Tom's nickname is California Cool. Like Montana, Tom is calm when the game is on the line. But Montana won four Super Bowls. Can Tom match that? He's giving it his best shot!